DESKTOP DOUBLES

Connie's computer screen is crowded with icons. Although they are in different places, all of the icons in two of the columns below are the same. Can you find the two columns with the same icons?

File Edit View Help

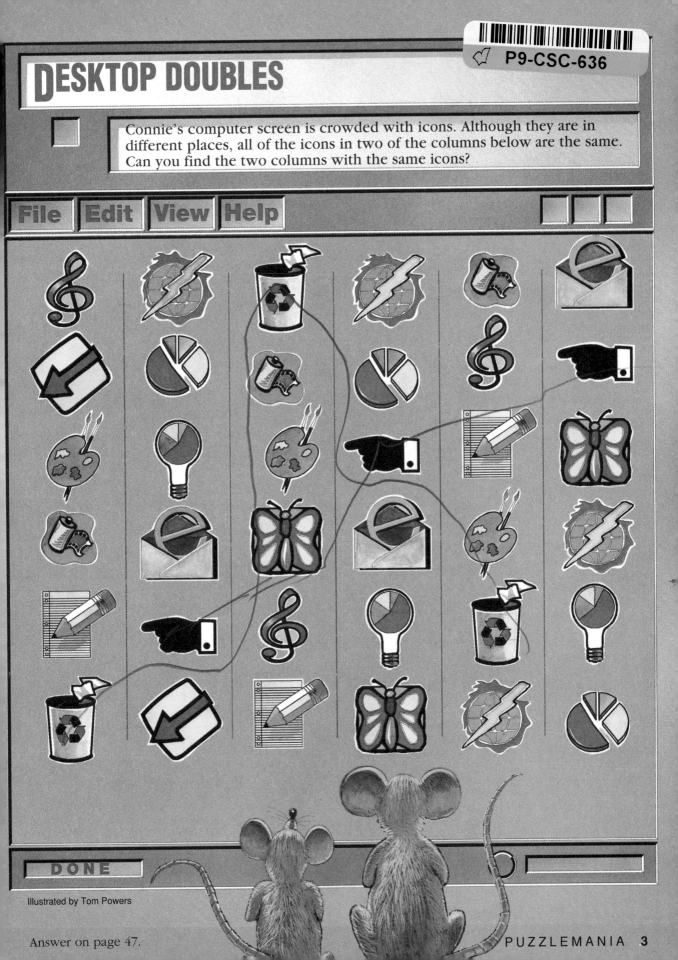

DONE

Illustrated by Tom Powers

Answer on page 47.

LOST AND FOUND

It's been a very busy day at the Lost-and-Found Desk. Can you help the clerk return the lost items to their owners? Which item will be left on the shelf?

Answer on page 47.

Oh *K!*

How many things in this picture begin with the letter *K?*

Answer on page 47.

HIDDEN PLANETS

The names of all nine planets are hidden in the letters below. Can you find them? Look up, down, across, and diagonally. Be careful—some words overlap, and some are written backward.

```
L M V E N U S O
R O E E A R T H
E S M R K A F P
T A O A C N L R
I T A P R U U R
P U P L T S R E
U R M O O O N Y
J N E P T U N E
```

Illustrated by Barbara Gray

Answer on page 47.

WALKING WIGGLY

Mark is taking his new pet, Wiggly, for a walk. What do you think it is? Use your imagination, and finish this picture.

Illustrated by Holly Kowitt

HOW MANY __ IN A __?

There are 60 s. in a m. That's a quick way to say 60 seconds in a minute. Now that you know the quick system, try these:

1. 3 f. in a y.
2. 7 d. in a w.
3. 4 q. in a g.
4. 12 m. in a y.
5. 12 i. in a f.
6. 2 c. in a p.
7. 60 m. in an h.
8. 365 d. in a y.
9. 24 h. in a d.
10. 52 w. in a y.

Illustrated by Jennifer Skopp

Answer on page 47.

CALL TO ORDER

These pictures are out of order. Can you number them so
they tell a story from beginning to end?

Illustrated by John Nez

Answer on page 47.

PICTURE CROSSWORD

These pictures tell you what word to write
in the spaces across ➡ and down ↓.

SEE WHAT SUE SAW

Sue uses her binoculars wherever she goes. Can you tell where she went each day?

Monday

Tennis

Tuesday

Baksetball

golf

Wednesday

Answer on page 48.

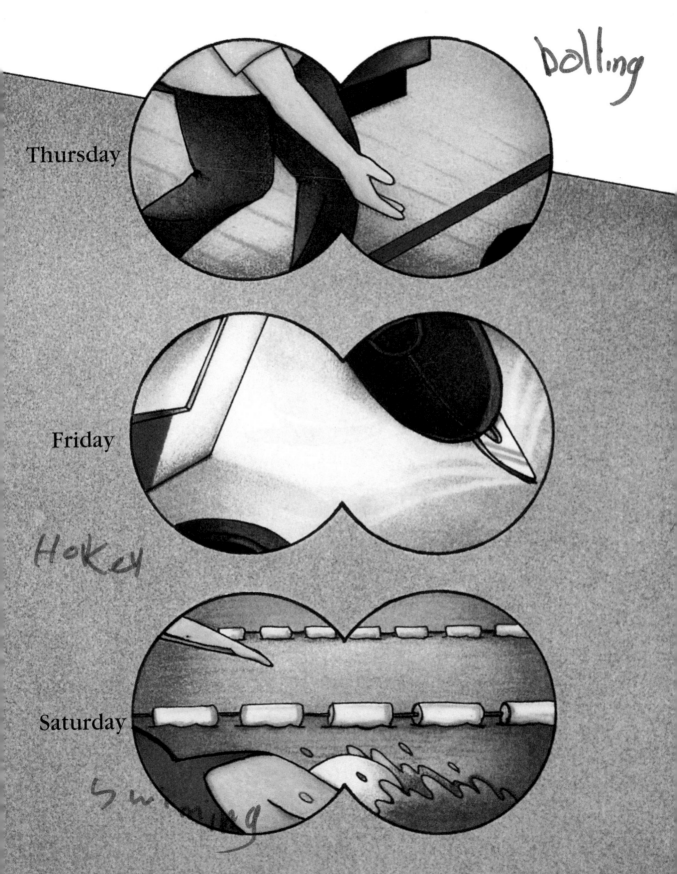

Thursday

Friday

Saturday

bowling

Hockey

swimming

MIX-UP AT THE CANDY COMPANY

There's been a mix-up at Alexandra's Candy Company. The barrels are numbered, but no one knows what's in them. The letters on the labels have been scrambled. The one labeled MARASCLE is actually full of CARAMELS. Help Alexandra unscramble the other candy names so she can get back to pulling taffy.

1. MARASCLE

2. FEOFET — *Jelly Beans*

3. CILROCIE — *Licorice*

4. MUGSPROD

5. LEJLY SNABE

6. LIPOSLOPL — *lollypops*

7. SWALLOMSHARM — *Marshmallows*

8. HEATCLOCO — *Chocolate*

9. DUGEF

10. TENAPU TRIBLET

Illustrated by Jerry Zimmerman

Answer on page 48.

HOP TO IT!

Harvey is hurrying home to his hutch. He needs
to pick up groceries along the way. There are
lots to choose from, but his family eats only raw
vegetables. Which way should Harvey go to find
foods that rabbits might like?

START

KOLA COLA

CANNED SOUP

HARVEY

FINISH

Illustrated by Barbara Gray

ALPHABEADS

Start at the top with *A*. Move up, down, left, right, or diagonally to the nearest *B*. From there, move to the nearest *C*. Connect the beads to make an alphabet necklace from *A* to *Z*.

START

D	A	L	W	F	J	K
K	N	B	R	D	I	O
M	C	D	K	F	G	A
P	I	R	E	B	H	X
R	S	J	X	M	K	I
F	H	F	O	T	J	O
M	O	Q	R	V	K	T
A	X	G	Q	L	B	K
F	T	M	F	W	M	P
U	O	D	N	X	F	N
V	M	B	R	S	O	L
R	I	X	S	Q	P	X
S	W	T	X	P	F	P
M	S	X	U	S	O	A
K	Y	V	S	N	U	G
R	V	W	J	X	D	M
T	N	X	W	I	I	J
M	Y	P	K	N	F	S
Z	M	T	L	R	B	E

FINISH

Illustrated by Jennifer Skopp

Answer on page 48.

JUNGLE MEMORIES
Part 1

Take a long look at this picture. Try to remember everything you see in it. Then turn the page and try to answer some questions about it without looking back.

DON'T READ THIS UNTIL YOU HAVE LOOKED AT "Jungle Memories-Part 1" ON PAGE 17.

JUNGLE MEMORIES
Part 2

Can you answer these questions about the jungle scene you saw?

1. How many elephants did you see?
2. Was the turtle swimming? *Yes*
3. Were all the animals right side up? *Yes*
4. Did the cat have stripes or spots? *Sp*
5. How many birds were on the vine? *Two*

6. Was the man holding an ice-cream cone or a cookie?
7. Which animal held a flower? *Monkey*
8. How many birds were flying? *zero*

Answer on page 48.

AT THE FINISH LINE

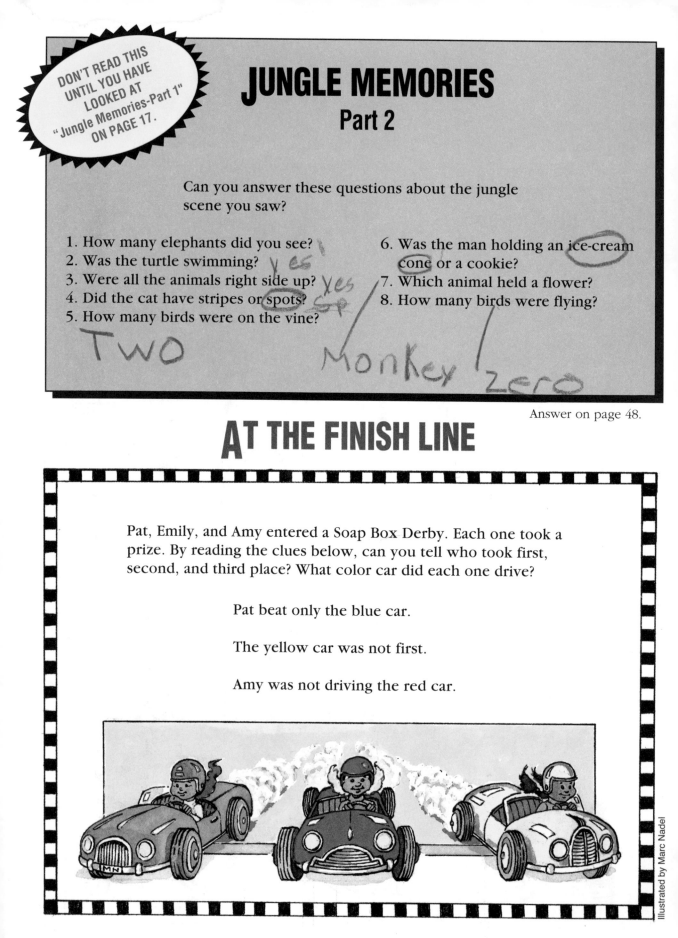

Pat, Emily, and Amy entered a Soap Box Derby. Each one took a prize. By reading the clues below, can you tell who took first, second, and third place? What color car did each one drive?

Pat beat only the blue car.

The yellow car was not first.

Amy was not driving the red car.

Illustrated by Marc Nadel

Answer on page 48.

ROW, ROW, ROW

Each of these students has something in common with the two others in the same row of pictures. You can see that all three students in the top row across are wearing shirts of the same color. Look at the other rows across, down, and diagonally. Can you tell what's alike in each row?

Answer on page 49.

TREASURE HUNT

Captain Richman keeps his treasure on a secret island. Starting at the ship, follow the directions on the map from island to island. When you find a letter, stash it away in the ship's locker. Once you reach Richman's Island, the letters will tell you what the captain keeps there.

CONEY ISLAND TAKE A "D" AND SAIL TO GRITTY ISLAND!

ITCHY ISLAND MOSQUITOS! GO EAST

SAIL ON NORTHEAST

FINISH

RICHMAN'S ISLAND

KITE ISLAND FLY NORTH TO ITCHY ISLAND

MOUSE ISLAND TAKE AN "H" GO NORTHEAST TO RICHMAN'S ISLAND

LETTER LOCKER

FIRE ISLAND TOO HOT GO EAST

★ START

ANGLE ISLAND GO EAST TO THE THIRD ISLAND

Illustrated by Terry Kovalcik

SOMETHING FISHY

There are at least ten differences in these two pictures. How many can you find?

WHAT A WAY TO GO!

These explorers are traveling across the country. To find out how they'll get there, connect the red dots from 1 to 31. Then connect the blue dots from A to Z. Bon voyage!

CROSSING THE STATES

The names of all fifty states fit into the spaces on the following page. The lists tell how many letters are in each state name. This will help you see where they fit into the puzzle. Some of the states have been filled in. It may help you to cross each state off the list when you put it in the puzzle.

4 LETTERS
IOWA
OHIO
UTAH

5 LETTERS
IDAHO
MAINE
TEXAS

6 LETTERS
ALASKA
HAWAII
KANSAS
NEVADA
OREGON

7 LETTERS
ALABAMA
ARIZONA
FLORIDA
GEORGIA
INDIANA
MONTANA
NEW YORK
VERMONT
WYOMING

8 LETTERS
ARKANSAS
COLORADO
DELAWARE
ILLINOIS
KENTUCKY
MARYLAND
MICHIGAN
MISSOURI
NEBRASKA
OKLAHOMA
VIRGINIA

9 LETTERS
LOUISIANA
MINNESOTA
NEW JERSEY
NEW MEXICO
TENNESSEE
WISCONSIN

10 LETTERS
CALIFORNIA
WASHINGTON

11 LETTERS
CONNECTICUT
MISSISSIPPI
NORTH DAKOTA
RHODE ISLAND
SOUTH DAKOTA

12 LETTERS
NEW HAMPSHIRE
PENNSYLVANIA
WEST VIRGINIA

13 LETTERS
MASSACHUSETTS
NORTH CAROLINA
SOUTH CAROLINA

UNITED STATES OF AMERICA

GULF OF MEXICO

ILLINOIS

PENNSYLVANIA

NORTHDAKOTA

SOUTHCAROLINA

MONTANA

ALASKA

Illustrated by Pat Merrell

SQUARE HUNT

Inside this big square are many smaller squares.
How many can you find altogether?

Answer on page 49.

Illustrated by Pat Merrell

THE SECRET LISTS

Webster and Wagnall both wanted the job of List Keeper to Queen Elistabeth. They each made a sample list. To keep their lists secret from each other, they both made up their own codes. Can you tell what's on each list and who wrote it?

This is Webster's code:

A = N	J = W	S = F
B = O	K = X	T = G
C = P	L = Y	U = H
D = Q	M = Z	V = I
E = R	N = A	W = J
F = S	O = B	X = K
G = T	P = C	Y = L
H = U	Q = D	Z = M
I = V	R = E	

This is Wagnall's code:

A = Z	J = Q	S = H
B = Y	K = P	T = G
C = X	L = O	U = F
D = W	M = N	V = E
E = V	N = M	W = D
F = U	O = L	X = C
G = T	P = K	Y = B
H = S	Q = J	Z = A
I = R	R = I	

Sea Creatures
1. WRYYLSVFU
2. JUNYR
3. CBECBVFR
4. QBYCUVA
5. BPGBCHF
6. FRNUBEFR
7. FGNESVFU
8. FDHVQ

Vegetables
1. XZFORUOLDVI
2. YVVG
3. YVZM
4. XZIILG
5. OVGGFXV
6. YILXXLOR
7. XLIM
8. XVOVIB

YO-YO U.

These freshmen at Yo-Yo University were studying for their first big test when this happened. Can you tell which yo-yo belongs to each student?

Answer on page 49.

SOUR NOTES

How many things can you find wrong in this picture?

M. Nadel

WORLD OF COLOR

These words are hidden in the letters you see
below. Look up, down, across, backward, and
diagonally. Some letters are used more than once.
When you find a word, circle it. After you finish,
put the leftover letters in the blank spaces to spell
a colorful message.

AQUA	GREEN	SILVER
BEIGE	HUE	SPECTRUM
BLACK	LIGHT	TAN
BLUE	ORANGE	TINT
BROWN	ORCHID	TRANSPARENT
COLOR WHEEL	PINK	TURQUOISE
DARK	PURPLE	VIBRANT
DULL	RED	VIOLET
GOLD	SHADE	WHITE
GRAY	SHINY	YELLOW

```
E   Y   E   L   L   O   W   A   L   T   R   S
T   R   A   N   S   P   A   R   E   N   T   P
I   A   E   I   N   A   T   B   E   I   R   E
H   N   B   D   G   Q   L   O   H   T   E   C
W   E   L   P   R   U   P   U   W   B   V   T
W   T   O   I   E   A   E   Y   R   E   L   R
V   H   R   N   E   O   A   O   O   I   I   U
I   G   C   K   N   R   W   K   L   G   S   M
O   I   H   E   G   N   A   R   O   E   D   D
L   L   I   F   C   B   L   A   C   K   L   U
E   O   D   L   S   H   A   D   E   O   O   L
T   U   R   Q   U   O   I   S   E   R   G   L
V   I   B   R   A   N   T   S   H   I   N   Y
```

Message:

‾‾ ‾‾‾‾ ‾‾‾ ‾‾‾ ‾‾‾ ‾‾‾ ‾‾‾ ‾‾‾ ‾‾‾

Answer on page 49.

Illustrated by Doug Taylor

PICKY'S PEACHES

Picky keeps his peach trees in perfect shape. In every row of trees, down, across, and diagonally, there are thirty peaches. Picky can tell how many peaches grow on each tree by the number of peaches on the corner trees. Can you?

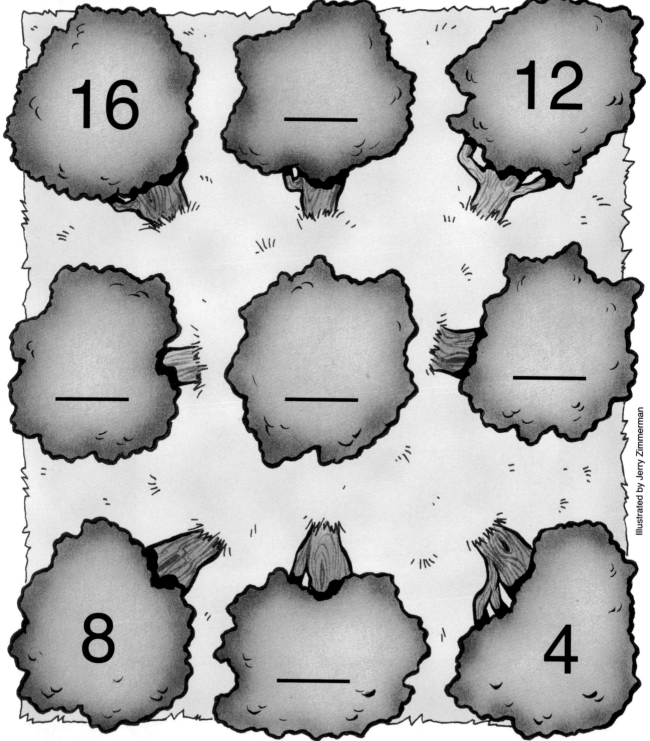

Answer on page 50.

ON THE GO

Look at these pictures. Write the words in the spaces next to them. When you finish, the letters in the yellow spaces will spell a long word. It means the way we move people and things from place to place.

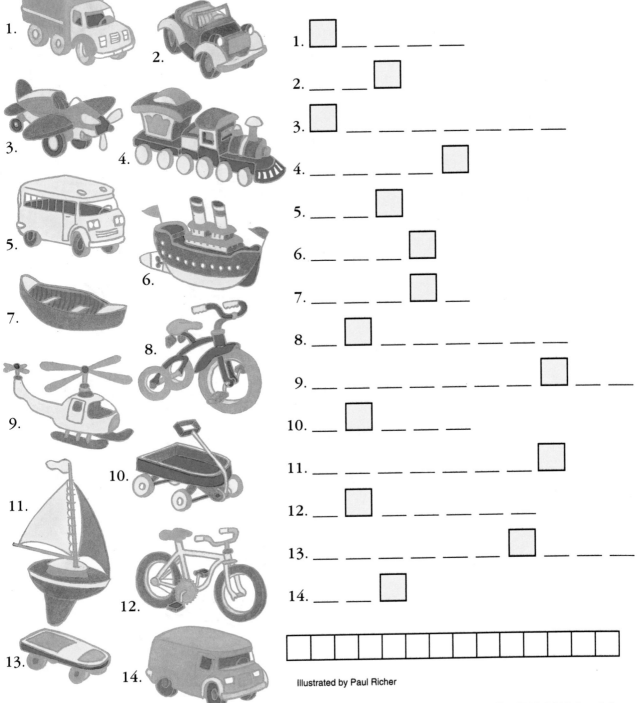

1. ☐ __ __ __ __

2. __ __ ☐

3. ☐ __ __ __ __ __ __ __

4. __ __ __ __ ☐

5. __ ☐

6. __ __ __ ☐

7. __ __ __ ☐ __

8. __ ☐ __ __ __ __ __ __

9. __ __ __ __ __ __ __ ☐ __ __

10. __ ☐ __ __ __

11. __ __ __ __ __ ☐

12. __ ☐ __ __ __ __

13. __ __ __ __ __ ☐ __ __

14. __ __ ☐

Illustrated by Paul Richer

Answer on page 50.

HIDDEN PICTURES™

There are at least eighteen objects hidden in this picture. How many can you find?

STACKING STUMPER

Mr. Stack, the lumberjack, has chopped a pile of wood.
Mr. Cross, his great big boss, said, "Straighten it up, if you could.
Put forty-five logs in every stack, and I will simply love it
If every row has one more log than the row above it."
How many logs in the bottom row?
That's what Mr. Stack needs to know.
Please help him figure out this mess.
Then turn to the answers and
check your guess.

Illustrated by Terry Kovalcik

Answer on page 50.

WHAT'S IN A WORD?

A lot of smaller words are skating around in the letters of SKATEBOARD. If you move some letters around, you'll find words like ASK and ROAD. How many words of three letters or more can you find? Proper names and plurals ending in *S* don't count. We found more than one hundred.

Illustrated by R. Michael Palan

Answer on page 50.

COMPUTER CRACK-UPS

Oops! Someone jiggled the giggle switch. Now the computer will do nothing but make riddles. Crack the coded answers and find out what's so funny.

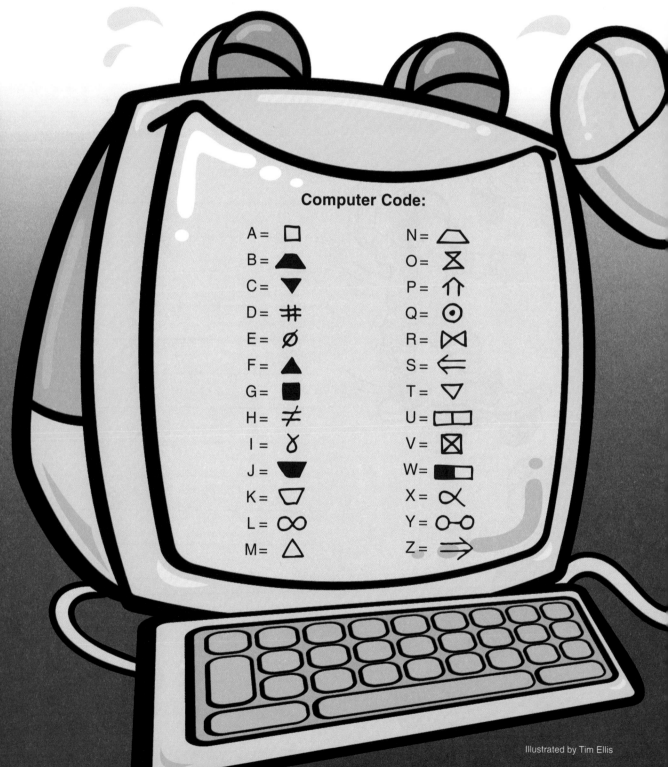

Computer Code:

A = □
B = ◢◣
C = ▽
D = #
E = ∅
F = ▲
G = ■
H = ≠
I = ✗
J = ▼
K = ▽
L = ∞
M = △

N = ⬯
O = ⊠
P = ⇑
Q = ⊙
R = ⋈
S = ⇐
T = ▽
U = ▭
V = ⊠
W = ▭
X = ∝
Y = ⊶
Z = ⇒

1. What can speak every language?

□ ◁ ∅ ▼ ≠ ⋈

2. What holds the moon up?

△ ⋈ ⋈ ◁ ▲ ∅ □ △ ⇐

3. What is a pig after it is three days old?

▲ ⋈ □□ ⋈ #□○─○⇐ ⋈∞#

4. Why did the crow sit on the telephone wire?

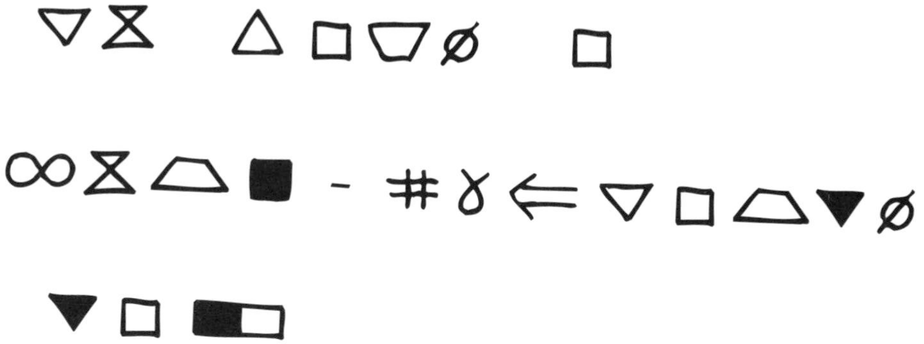

▽⋈ △□▽∅ □

∞⋈◁■ - #γ⇐▽□◁▼∅

▼□ ■□

MEALTIME AT THE ZOO

When it's suppertime, the zookeeper knows what everyone likes to eat.
Can you match these animals with the foods they ask for in the poem
that follows?

giraffe	elephant	seal	human	monkey
parrot	squirrel	rabbit	beaver	tiger

1. _____ I earn fresh fish for doing my tricks.

2. _____ I chew the bark off stacks of sticks.

3. _____ Hay helps my trunk grow very strong.

4. _____ I nibble bananas all the day long.

5. _____ A bowl of salad is dinner to me.

6. _____ I find my meals at the top of a tree.

7. _____ I like steak and many other meats.

8. _____ Acorns and nuts are my special treats.

9. _____ A pile of seeds fills up my belly.

10. _____ I munch on peanut butter and jelly!

Illustrated by Jerry Zimmerman

Answer on page 50.

PUPPY PUZZLE

Cara, John, Ryan, and Diane have each chosen a puppy at the animal shelter. Look at the picture, and read the clues. Can you tell which puppy belongs to which dog lover?

1. Diane didn't want a puppy with spots.
2. Ryan didn't choose a puppy with a collar.
3. John didn't pick a puppy that's sleeping.
4. Cara took a puppy that John and Diane did not want.

Illustrated by John Nez

NOODLES

SPOTTY

PATCHES

WINKY

Answer on page 50.

ALL ABOUT ANIMALS

How well do you know animals? Fill in the blanks and see.

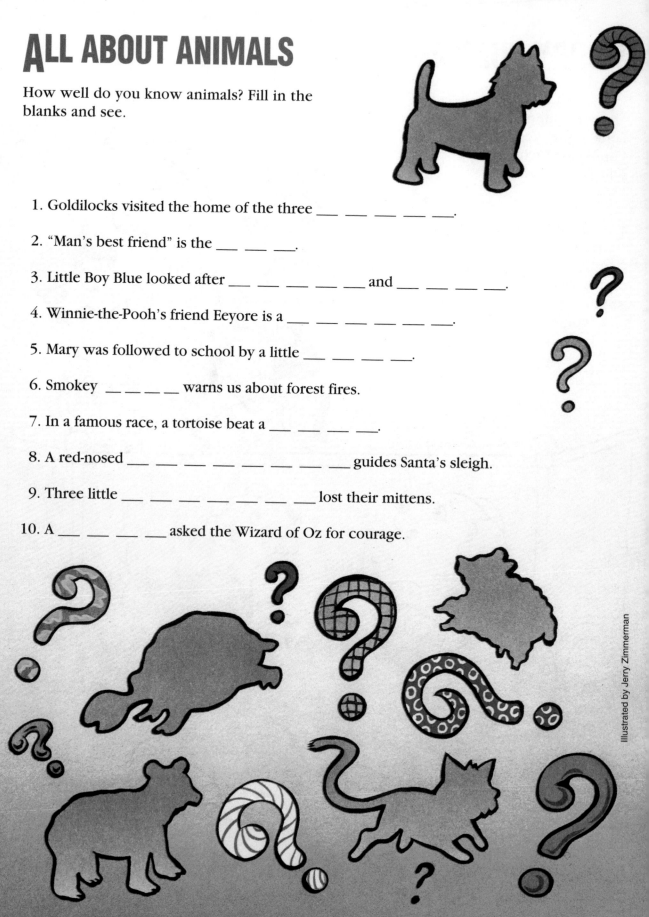

1. Goldilocks visited the home of the three __ __ __ __ __.

2. "Man's best friend" is the __ __ __.

3. Little Boy Blue looked after __ __ __ __ __ and __ __ __ __.

4. Winnie-the-Pooh's friend Eeyore is a __ __ __ __ __ __.

5. Mary was followed to school by a little __ __ __ __.

6. Smokey __ __ __ __ warns us about forest fires.

7. In a famous race, a tortoise beat a __ __ __ __.

8. A red-nosed __ __ __ __ __ __ __ __ guides Santa's sleigh.

9. Three little __ __ __ __ __ __ __ lost their mittens.

10. A __ __ __ __ asked the Wizard of Oz for courage.

Answer on page 50.

STOP, LOOK, AND LIST

Under each category list one thing that begins with each letter. For example, one sport that begins with *S* is SOFTBALL. See if you can name another.

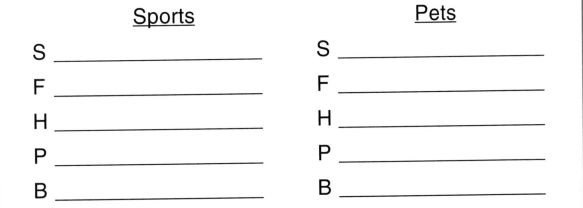

Sports

S _____

F _____

H _____

P _____

B _____

Pets

S _____

F _____

H _____

P _____

B _____

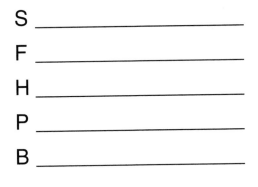

Musical Instruments

S _____

F _____

H _____

P _____

B _____

Answer on page 50.   Illustrated by Doug Taylor

OFF THE TOP OF YOUR HEAD

Use your imagination and finish drawing
the costume-contest winners.

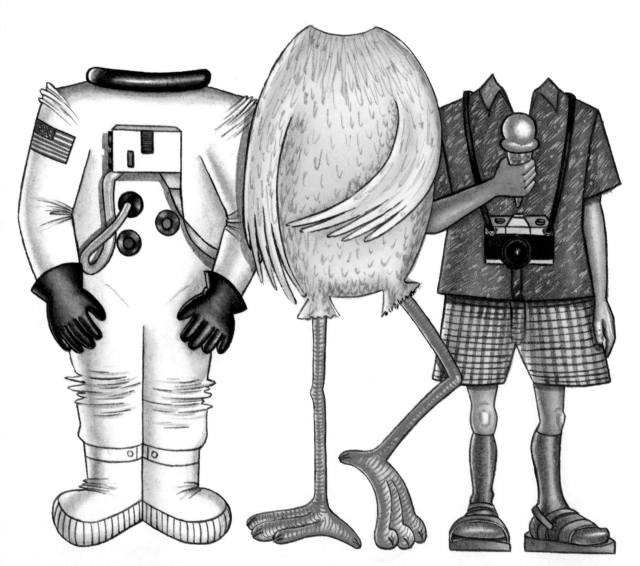

Illustrated by Jennifer Skopp

ROVING ROBOT

All the robots are in their places except the one in the center. Can you program its way to the empty corner?

FINISH

START

Illustrated by Jennifer Skopp

Answer on page 50.